Archie Dare

BY

Pen

the

devil

ANDY

RASH

guin

VIKING
An Imprint of Penguin Group (USA)

Hey Archie! Let's all swim over to Iceberg Nine and have a fish fry!

Swim? No thanks, fellows.
If my latest invention works, I'll fly over!

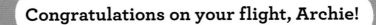

Congratulations on your flight, Archie!

How far did I go, Mr. Mayor?

You flew twenty feet straight down!

Hmmm. Still not good enough. I need more thrust.

Zounds! My rocket has melted the ice, setting me adrift in the sea! HELP! HELLLP!
Just swim, Archie! SWIM!
HISS
GLUB
GLUB
GLUB

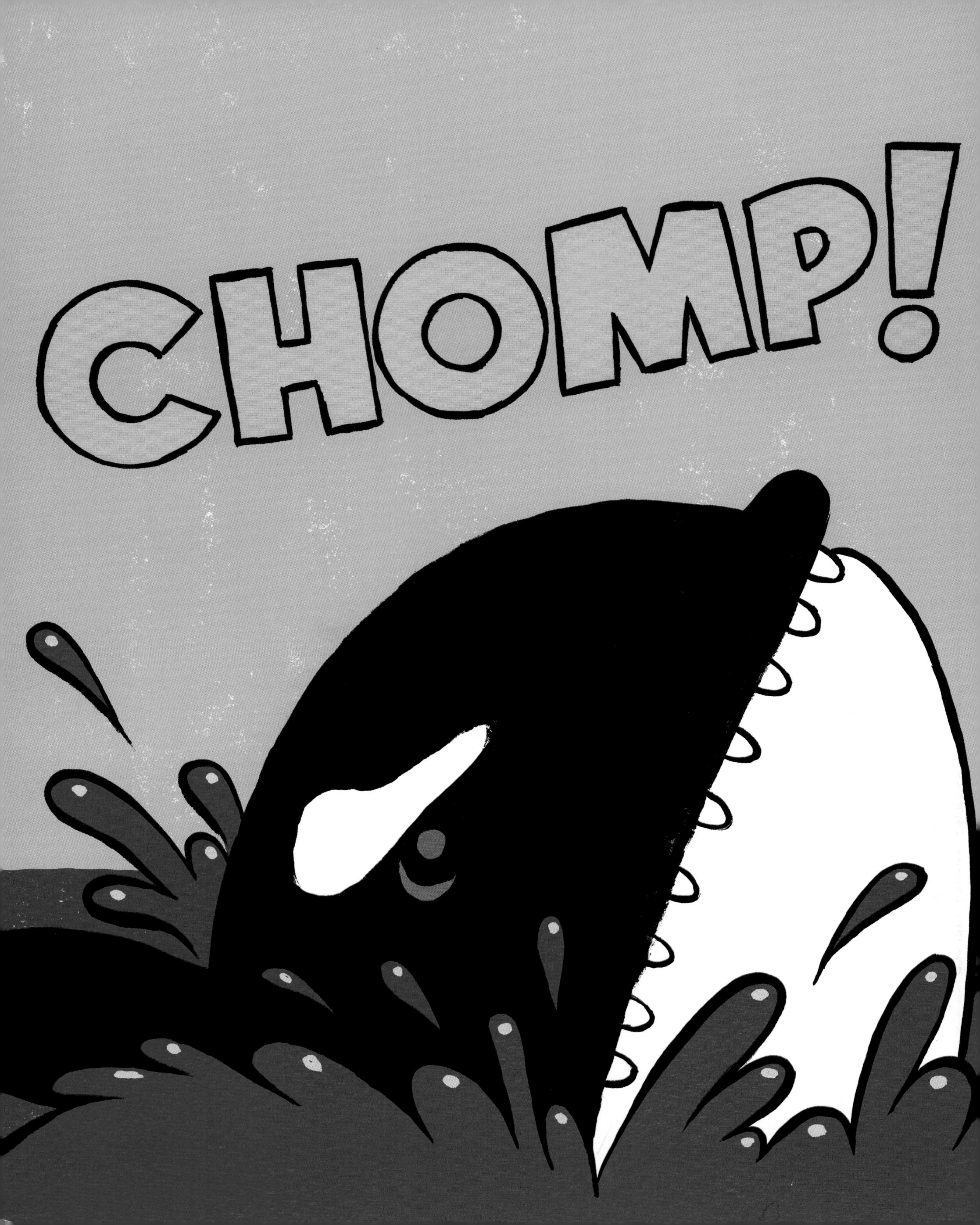
CHOMP!

What a glorious feeling!
I can see my igloo from here!
The sun!
The wind!

Whoops! Losing a little altitude here.
FLAP FLAP FLAP
That doesn't help! Mayday! Mayday!

SPLASH!

Oh yeah. That was pretty fun, too. Can we go for another swim?
Sure!
MAYOR

VIKING
Published by the Penguin Group
Penguin Group (USA) LLC
375 Hudson Street
New York, New York 10014

USA * Canada * UK * Ireland * Australia
New Zealand * India * South Africa * China

penguin.com
A Penguin Random House Company

First published in the United States of
America by Viking, an imprint of
Penguin Young Readers Group, 2015

LIBRARY OF CONGRESS CATALOGING-IN-PUBLICATION DATA IS AVAILABLE
ISBN: 978-0-451-47123-9

1   2   3   4   5   6   7   8   9   10

Manufactured in China   Set in Archer Bold   Book design by Andy Rash

For Joe and Katie